Whistling for Angela

BY Robin Heald

ILLUSTRATED BY

Peggy Collins

First published in Canada and the United States in 2022

Text copyright © 2022 Robin Heald

Illustration copyright © 2022 Peggy Collins

This edition copyright © 2022 Pajama Press Inc.

This is a first edition.

10 9 8 7 6 5 4 3 2 1

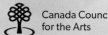 Canada Council Conseil des arts
for the Arts du Canada

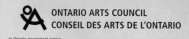 ONTARIO ARTS COUNCIL
CONSEIL DES ARTS DE L'ONTARIO
an Ontario government agency
un organisme du gouvernement de l'Ontario

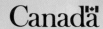 Canadä

Library and Archives Canada Cataloguing in Publication
Title: Whistling for Angela / by Robin Heald ; illustrated Peggy Collins.
Names: Heald, Robin, 1954- author. | Collins, Peggy, 1975- illustrator.
Identifiers: Canadiana 2021030507X | ISBN 9781772782455 (hardcover)
Classification: LCC PZ7.H34352 Whi 2022 | DDC j813/.6—dc23

Publisher Cataloging-in-Publication Data (U.S.)

Names: Heald, Robin, 1954-, author. | Collins, Peggy, 1975-, illustrator.
Title: Whistling for Angela / by Robin Heald ; illustrated by Peggy Collins.
Description: Toronto, Ontario Canada : Pajama Press, 2022. | Summary: "Daniel loves birds, and wants
to learn how to whistle as a gift for his new adoptive baby sister Angela. On the day they bring her home,
Daniel still can't whistle. It is through meeting Jessie, Angela's birthmother, that Daniel may learn the trick
to whistle like the birds he loves"— Provided by publisher.
Identifiers: ISBN 978-1-77278-245-5 (hardcover)
Subjects: LCSH: Adopted children – Family relationships – Juvenile fiction. | Birdsongs -- Juvenile fiction.
| Brothers and sisters – Juvenile fiction. | BISAC: JUVENILE FICTION / Family / Adoption. | JUVENILE
FICTION / Family / New Baby. | JUVENILE FICTION / Family / Siblings.
Classification: LCC PZ7.H435Wh |DDC [F] – dc23
Original art created digitally
Cover and book design—Lorena González Guillén

Manufactured in China by WKT Company

Pajama Press Inc.

11 Davies Avenue, Suite 103, Toronto, Ontario Canada, M4M 2A9

Distributed in Canada by UTP Distribution
5201 Dufferin Street Toronto, Ontario Canada, M3H 5T8

Distributed in the U.S. by Ingram Publisher Services
1 Ingram Blvd. La Vergne, TN 37086, USA

For Dylan and Zoë
and their birth mothers,
Pam and Becky

—R.H.

For my mom and dad

—P.C.

"I'm going to learn to whistle for the new baby," said Daniel.
"It'll be my present to her. I'll whistle like a bird."

"Whistling's hard with no front teeth," Dad said.

But to Daniel, whistling was the best sound ever. And the chickadee's *fee bee* call had just two whistles.
"I can do it!" he said.

"We leave for the adoption center bright and early tomorrow," Dad said. "Better get started."

Daniel tried whistling:

Outside... **PHWWWT!**

No whistle, just air and spit.

At lunch...

PFPFPFPF!

"Whoa! Spinach spray!" said Dad.

While Mom put together the baby's crib, Daniel looked through his feather collection. His prize feather was from a blue jay and he took it everywhere.

"Does Angela like birds?" he asked.

"She's only four months old. She'll grow to love them because you love them," Mom said.

"Will she love me?" Daniel asked.

Mom kissed his cheek. "Babies love people who make them feel loved."

Daniel knew a lot about birds. Feathers and hollow bones helped them fly. Some birds migrated a long way for the winter. And birds built nests so their babies would be safe.

About babies he knew just a little. They wore diapers, and they couldn't walk or talk. If they weren't happy, they cried.

Whistling like a bird made Daniel happy. It would make the baby happy too.

At bedtime Daniel said, "Mom, tell me again."

"Some babies grow inside their moms," Mom said, "and when they're born they stay in that family forever. Some babies grow inside their birth mothers, then they're adopted by a new family and stay in that family forever."

Two friends in Daniel's class were adopted. Kira had been born in China. She didn't know her birth mother. Oliver FaceTimed with his birth mother.

Angela had grown inside her birth mother, Jessie. Tomorrow Daniel and his family would meet them both.

The next morning, Daniel practiced whistling:

In the car...He sounded like a cat hissing.

In the parking lot...He sounded like a spooky ghost.

His present wasn't *near* ready.

Time was running out.

At the adoption center, Daniel was allowed to go into the hallway. Mom and Dad were talking to the adoption counselor, the person whose job it was to help families grow.

The hallway was echoey and longer than a bowling lane.

Daniel blew and puffed and panted. **NO WHISTLE**.

"Hey, there!" called a voice. "Are you Daniel?"

He spun around. "Uh-huh!"

A lady was standing there with a baby in her arms. "I'm Jessie. This is Angela."

"Mom! Dad!" Daniel yelled. "Our baby's here! She's almost bald!"

The grown-ups took turns holding Angela.
She put their presents in her mouth.
No smiles.

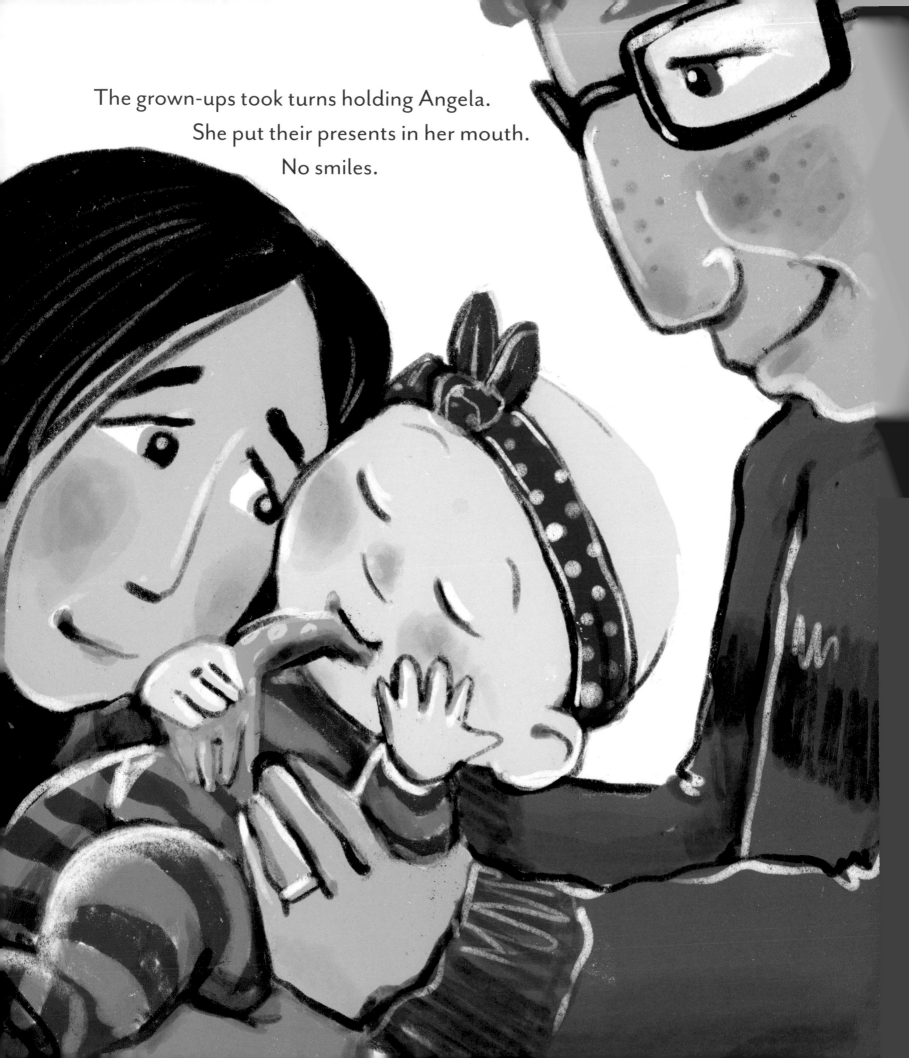

It was time for Daniel's present.

"I'd like to hold Angela," he announced.

"Baby bird coming in for a landing," said Jessie.

"You like birds?" Daniel asked.

"They're magical," Jessie said. "I have three parakeets: Peter, Piper, and Peck."

Daniel made his lap and his arms sturdy like a bird's nest to keep his sister safe.

Daniel had never held a baby before. Angela felt
warm and soft. Her head smelled like vanilla cookies.

"Your present's inside me." Daniel whispered.
"You can't put it in your mouth."

Daniel pretended he was blowing out birthday candles.
PHWEEEET! No whistle.

He blew one long stream...of air. No whistle.

"Daniel, here's the secret to whistling," Jessie said. "Pretend you're tasting a lemon. Pucker your mouth to make lemon lips, and leave a hole so tiny that Angela can't even fit in her pinky. Then blow."

Daniel breathed in, puckered his lips, and...

THUMP! Angela's head!
"OWWW!" Daniel's chin!

Angela wailed.

Daniel's chin stung.

Jessie reached for Angela.

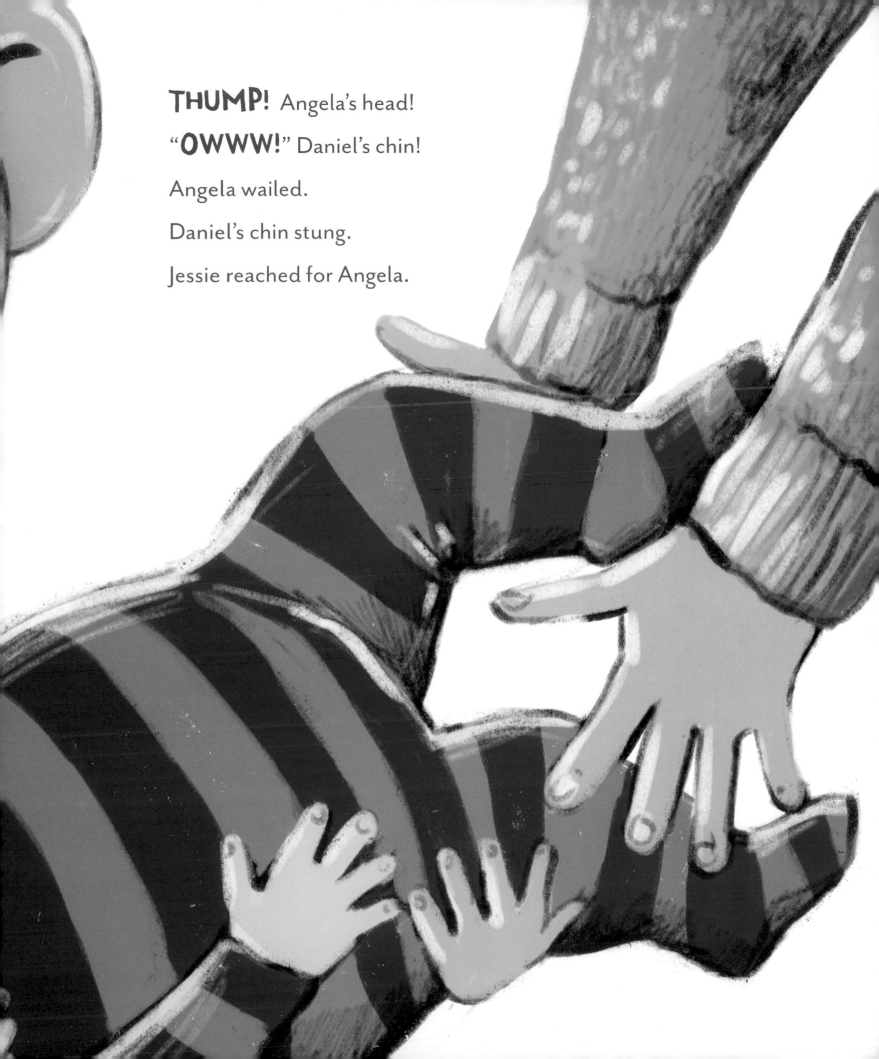

"Wait!" Daniel filled his lungs, made lemon lips, and blew gently. And this time, a soft whistle came out. A real whistle!

Angela stopped crying.

Everyone cheered.

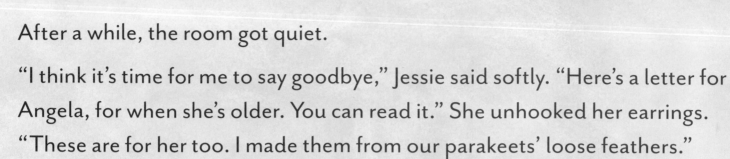

After a while, the room got quiet.

"I think it's time for me to say goodbye," Jessie said softly. "Here's a letter for Angela, for when she's older. You can read it." She unhooked her earrings. "These are for her too. I made them from our parakeets' loose feathers."

Daniel saw tears on Jessie's cheeks.

He didn't feel like whistling anymore.

"You'll always be part of Angela's life," said Mom.

"We're grateful to you, Jessie," said Dad.

Everyone hugged. Jessie snuggled Angela and settled her in Mom's arms.

And then she left.

"Why can't Angela stay with Jessie?"
Daniel asked.

Mom read Jessie's letter to herself.
"She talks about why in
this letter. Listen."

Dear Angela,
Always remember that I
Love you. I want you to
have the best life possible,
a life I wish I could give
you. I've chosen wonderful
parents for you, and an
awesome brother. I will
think of you every day.
your birth mother,
Jessie

This was a happy day because Daniel was a big brother—Jessie had chosen him. And he'd learned to whistle—Jessie had taught him. But it was a sad day too. Jessie had said goodbye to Angela, and she loved her. Daniel wanted to help Jessie feel better. But how?

Daniel charged down the hall to Jessie.

"This is for you." Daniel said. "It's from a blue jay."

Jessie took the feather in her hand. "It's beautiful."

"Your other present's inside me," said Daniel. "It's a promise-present.
I'm going to take really good care of Angela, and so will Mom and Dad.
They practiced on me."

"They did a wonderful job," said Jessie.

"And...I'll teach Angela about birds," Daniel went on, "because you love them and I love them and she will too. We'll all share the same bird love."

"You're good at sharing love," said Jessie. "You make *me* feel loved. Goodbye, Bird Boy."

"There you are!" Mom said. "Ready to go?"

"Ready, Angela?" said Daniel.

Then Daniel took a deep breath...and whistled the prettiest sound he knew: the chickadee's *fee bee* song.

Angela cooed...
and smiled.

♪ fee Bee

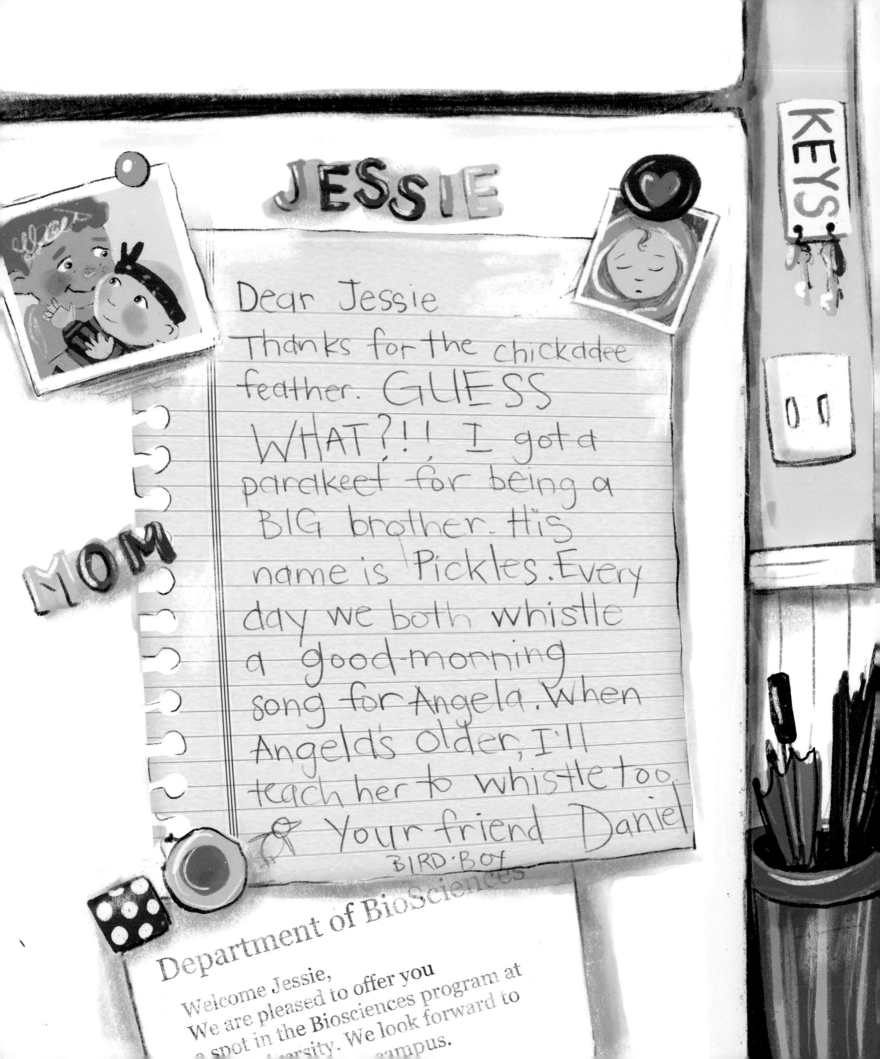

Author's Note

The adoption journey is near and dear to me. I was adopted by my father, and my husband and I adopted both our children, who are now grown.

Whistling for Angela was inspired by something that really happened on the day we met our daughter, Zoë. Right after we said goodbye to Zoë's birth mother, our son, Dylan, ran after her. Later, I asked Dylan what he'd said. "I told her that she shouldn't worry, because we'd take good care of the baby."

Dylan's words planted the seed for this picture book. I knew I wanted to tell the story of a birth mother meeting the adoptive family she has chosen. I wanted to show not only the excitement and joy of welcoming a baby into a family, but also the sad part, when the baby's birth mother says goodbye. I wanted to honor birth mothers who have made an adoption plan, which may be the hardest decision of their lives.

It's not always possible for birth parents and adoptive parents to meet and to have contact throughout their lives. But if it is possible, it can be helpful to everyone in the *adoption triangle:* the child, the birth parent(s), and the adoptive parent(s). Children can hear from their birth parents that they are loved. They can learn why staying with their first family was not possible. Birth parents are comforted, not needing to wonder what became of the child. And as an adoptive parent, knowing our children's birth mothers has expanded our sense of family. They are loved and valued because they are a part of our children.

My hope is that children and adults reading *Whistling for Angela* will embrace how all families are formed. What counts most in a family is love.

–Robin Heald